A NOTE ABOUT THIS STORY

You may have noticed that the usual counting book goes to ten. Prepare yourself for the unusual, because crows can't count that high and this story is based on fact. According to an experiment some hunters conducted many years ago, crows are pretty good at counting. This story is based on that experiment.

For all my teachers
and yours, too!
—A. W.

For Katherine Hale Apostolou
(our new baby, Kate)
—C. H.

Those Calculating CROWS!

BY **Ali Wakefield**

PICTURES BY **Christy Hale**

Simon & Schuster Books for Young Readers

On Sunday, the sweet corn started to sprout.

On Monday, Roy saw one crow fly over the farm pond.

By Tuesday, a whole flock of crows
was eating Roy's tender, sweet corn sprouts!
Roy and Dot had to stop those hungry crows!

Roy said, "Dot, I've got an idea! I'll chase those crows out of my garden, then I'll hide in the tool shed and wait for them to return. When they do, I'll take my gun and fire it into the air, KABOOM! The noise will scare those pesky crows away from our corn patch for good!"

Caw! The big guard crow saw Roy heading for the garden. He warned the others, and off they all flew.

Roy went into the tool shed to wait for the crows to return. Roy waited ten minutes. Roy waited twenty minutes. But the crows did not fly back.

Where were those pesky crows?

"Could it be crows count on their toes?" Roy wondered.

Roy waited, and he waited some more.

Still, no crows.

"Crows are too dumb to count to ONE," thought Roy.

Finally, when it was time for lunch, Roy went home.

And the crows came back.

Dot had an idea. "Maybe," she said, "we could fool the crows if we go out to the tool shed together. In five minutes, I'll come back, but you stay and wait for the crows. The crows will see me go inside the house, and they'll think it's safe to land in the garden."

"Yes," said Roy. "Then I'll take my gun and KABOOM! Those pesky crows will stay away from my corn patch for good!"

So Dot and Roy went outside and walked toward the tool shed. *Caw, caw!* The big guard crow warned the other crows and off they all flew.

TWO huddled in the tool shed together.

After five minutes, ONE left and slowly
walked back to the house.

Roy waited ten minutes. Roy waited twenty minutes.
But the crows did not fly back.

**Where were those
pesky crows?**

"Could it be crows count on
their toes?" Roy wondered.
Roy waited, and he waited some more.
Still no crows!
"Crows are not dumb. They count to
ONE! But it couldn't be true that crows
count to TWO!" said Roy.
Finally, when it was time for dinner,
Roy went home.
And the crows came back.

That night, Roy said, "It's a good idea, Dot, but we need more people."

After dinner Dot got it all arranged.

On Wednesday morning, the crows were back in Roy's sweet corn patch before sunrise. Helen arrived after breakfast and Roy, Dot, and Dot's friend Helen walked to the tool shed.

The guard crow warned the other crows and off they all flew.

THREE huddled in the tool shed together.

After five minutes, TWO walked slowly
back to the house.

Where were
those pesky
crows?

Roy waited ten minutes. Roy waited twenty minutes.
But the crows did not fly back.

"Could it be crows count on their toes?"
Roy waited, and he waited some more.
Still no crows!
"Crows are not dumb, they count to ONE.
It must be true, a few count to TWO. But
can it be that crows count to THREE?"
Finally, when it was time for lunch, Roy
went home.
And the crows came back.

After lunch, Helen called her son, Ed, and asked him to come to
Roy's farm. When Ed arrived, Roy explained Dot's idea to fool the crows.

Ed thought it was a good plan, so Roy, Dot, Helen, and Ed walked
out to the tool shed together.

The guard crow warned the other crows and off they all flew.

Caw! Caw! Caw! Caw!

FOUR huddled in the tool shed together.

After five minutes, THREE left and slowly
walked back to the house.

Roy waited ten minutes. He waited twenty minutes.
But the crows did not fly back.

**Where were
those pesky
crows?**

"Could it be crows count on their toes?"

Roy waited, and he waited some more.

Still no crows!

"Crows are not dumb, they count to ONE. It must be true, a few count to TWO. It has to be, some crows count to THREE. But surely no more! Crows can't count to FOUR!"

Finally, when it was time for dinner, Roy went home.

And the crows came back.

Roy was discouraged. It had taken the crows only two days to eat half the tender corn sprouts in his garden. Did Roy give up? No! Roy went to town to buy more seed to replant the sweet corn patch. And he decided that he would need FIVE people to fool those pesky crows.

On Thursday, Dot got it all arranged. Roy, Dot, Helen, Ed, and Ed's friend Jimmy walked out to the tool shed.

The guard crow warned the other crows and off they all flew.

Caw! Caw! Caw! Caw! Caw!

FIVE huddled in the tool shed together.

After five minutes, FOUR left and slowly
walked back to the house.

Roy waited ten minutes.
He waited twenty minutes.
But the crows
did not fly back.

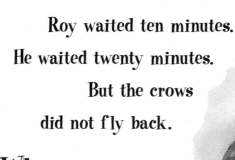

Where were
those pesky
crows?

"Could it be crows count on their toes?"

Roy waited, and he waited some more. **Still no crows!**

"Crows are not dumb, they count to ONE. It must be true, a few count to TWO. It has to be, crows count to THREE. And, what's more, some count to FOUR. But no crow alive can count to FIVE!"

Finally, when it was time for dinner, Roy went home. And the crows came back.

Ed and Jimmy called after dinner. "Did we fool the crows?" they asked. Roy told the boys what had happened, and they promised to bring Jimmy's sister, Susie, the next morning. "That will make SIX," Roy said. "Just what we need to fool those pesky crows. Come early!"

On Friday, Helen, Ed, Jimmy, and Susie knocked at the back door at eight o'clock.

"Come in, come in," said Roy. Dot made pancakes while the group reviewed the plan.

Roy, Dot, Helen, Ed, Jimmy, and Susie walked out to the garden.

The guard crow warned the other crows and off they all flew.

Caw! Caw! Caw! Caw! Caw! Caw!

SIX huddled together in the tool shed.

After five minutes, FIVE left and slowly
walked back to the house.

Roy waited ten minutes.
He waited twenty minutes.
But the crows did not fly back.

**Where were
those pesky
crows?**

"Could it be crows count on their toes?"
Roy waited, and he waited some more.
Still no crows!
"Crows are not dumb, they count to ONE.
It must be true, a few count to TWO. It has to be,
that crows count to THREE. And, what's more,
some count to FOUR. A few alive can count to FIVE.
But fiddlesticks! Crows can't count to SIX!"
Finally, when it was time for lunch, Roy went home.
And the crows came back.

Roy, Dot, Helen, Ed, Jimmy, and Susie sat at the kitchen table and ate their cheese sandwiches quietly. They watched the crows from the kitchen window.

The crows were eating their lunch, too. Roy groaned. Suddenly he sat up. "Troops," he said, "we can't give up! We need SEVEN next and if that doesn't work, we'll have to try EIGHT! Can you come back this afternoon?"

Caw! Caw! Caw!
Caw! Caw! Caw! Caw!

Later in the day, Roy, Dot, Helen, Ed, Jimmy, Susie, and Susie's friend Jill walked to the tool shed.

Roy was at the end of his rope. But did he give up? No!

On Saturday morning, Roy, Dot, Helen, Ed, Jimmy, Susie, Jill, and Jill's brother, Pete, walked out to the tool shed.

The guard crow warned the other crows and off they all flew.

Caw! Caw! Caw! Caw! Caw! Caw! Caw!

EIGHT huddled in the tool shed together.

After five minutes, SEVEN left and slowly walked back to the house, leaving Roy to wait for the crows all by himself.

He waited ten minutes.
He waited twenty minutes.
But the crows did not fly back.

"Could it be crows count on their toes?" Roy waited, and he waited some more.

Still, no crows!

"Crows are not dumb, they count to ONE. It must be true, a few count to TWO. It has to be, that crows count to THREE. And, what's more, some count to FOUR. A few alive can count to FIVE. By using tricks, crows count to SIX. And yes, good heaven, some count to SEVEN.

I'll have to wait. They may be late, but surely crows can't count to EIGHT!"

Just then,
the crows came back!

KABOOM!

KABOOM!

KABOOM!

And Roy took his gun and KABOOM! KABOOM!
Those pesky crows flew away and stayed out of
Roy's corn patch for good!

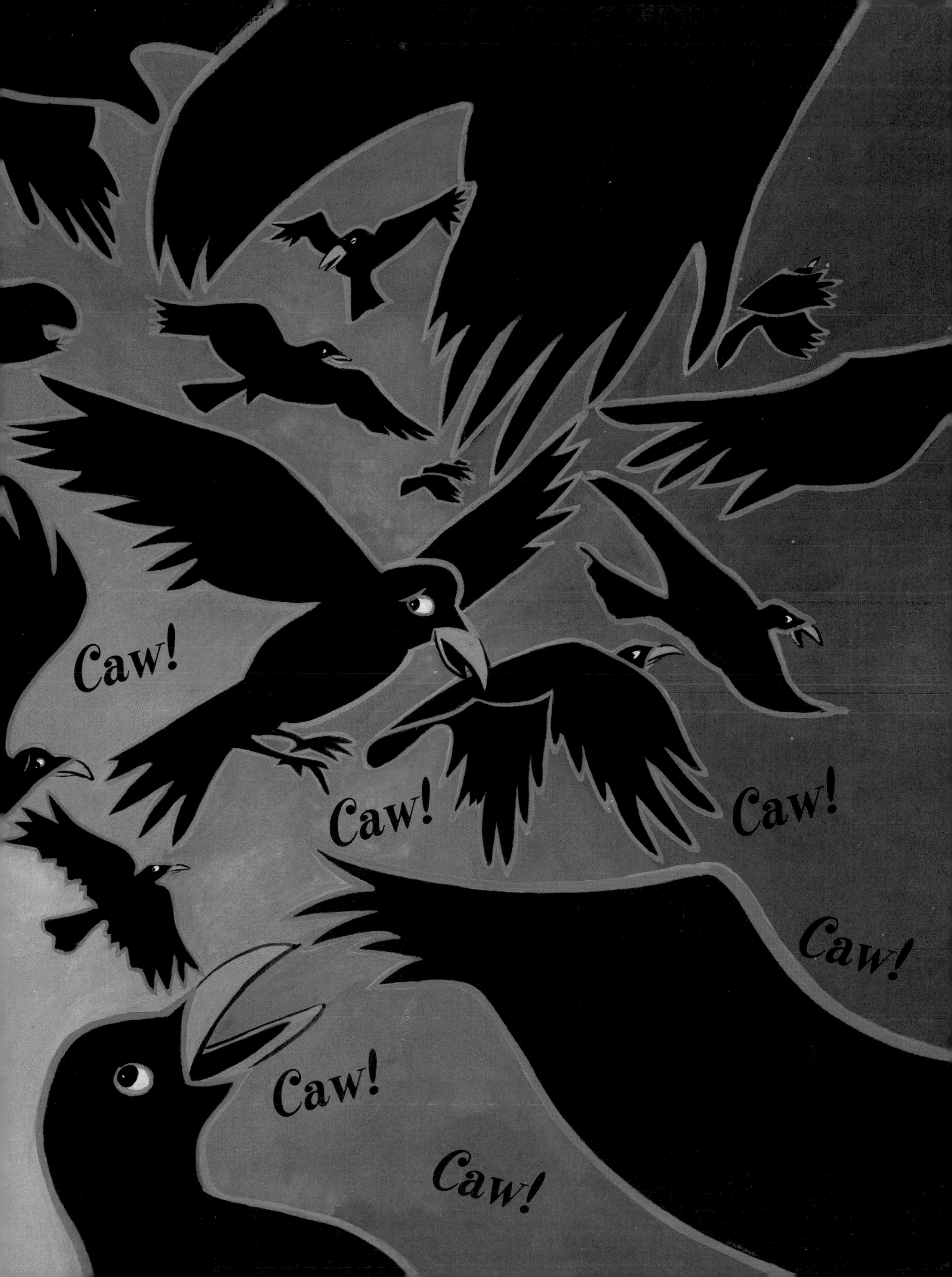
Caw!
Caw!
Caw!
Caw!
Caw!
Caw!

SIMON & SCHUSTER BOOKS FOR YOUNG READERS An imprint of Simon & Schuster Children's Publishing Division, 1230 Avenue of the Americas, New York, New York 10020

Text copyright © 1996 by Alice P. Wakefield. Illustrations copyright © 1996 by Christy Hale. All rights reserved including the right of reproduction in whole or in part in any form.
SIMON & SCHUSTER BOOKS FOR YOUNG READERS is a trademark of Simon & Schuster. Book design by Paul Zakris. The text for this book is set in 16-point Heatwave. The illustrations are rendered in gouache.
Printed and bound in Hong Kong by South China Printing Co. (1988) Ltd.
First Edition
10 9 8 7 6 5 4 3 2 1
LIBRARY OF CONGRESS CATALOGING-IN-PUBLICATION DATA
Wakefield, Alice P.
Those calculating crows! / by Alice P. Wakefield ; pictures by Christy Hale. – 1st ed.
    p.   cm.
Summary: When Roy tries to keep a flock of crows away from his
corn crop, it appears that these birds know how to count.
ISBN 0-689-80483-0
[1. Crows–Fiction. 2. Counting.] I. Hale, Christy, ill. II. Title.
PZ7.W13335Th 1996
[E]–dc20 95-30022